D1146890

Sshh!

For Julia

First published in 2001 by
Orion Children's Books
a division of the Orion Publishing Group
Orion House
5 Upper St Martin's Lane
London WC2H 9EA

Text and illustrations © Tony Kenyon 2001

The right of Tony Kenyon to be identified as
the author and illustrator of this work has been asserted.

All rights reserved. No part of this publication may be reproduced,
stored in a retrieval system, or transmitted, in any form or by any means, electronic,
mechanical, photocopying, recording or otherwise,
without the prior permission of Orion Children's Books.

A catalogue record for this book is available from the British Library.

Printed and bound in Italy by Printer Trento S.r.l.

Oops!
says Olly Bear

TONY KENYON

Orion
Children's Books

Olly Bear couldn't sleep.

He wiggled

and jiggled

and fell out of bed. OOPS!

"Something went BUMP!"
said Olly's mum.

"It's the front gate banging in the wind," said Olly's dad.

Olly climbed back into bed.

But he wanted a drink of milk.

He got out of bed again

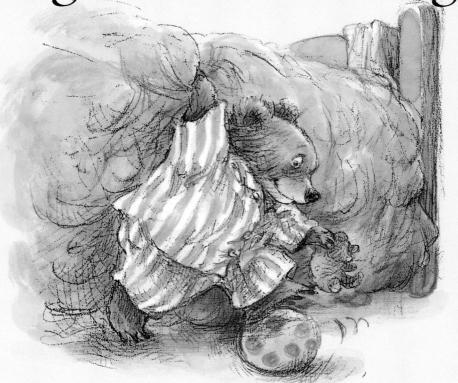

and slipped.

OOPS!

"What was that?" said Mum.
"I didn't hear anything,"
said Dad.

Olly tiptoed downstairs.

He had a glass of milk
and some chocolate cake.

BANG! went the
fridge door.
OOPS!

"That was a BANG!" said Mum.
"Quiet, I'm trying to sleep,"
said Dad.

Olly went back upstairs.

He got into bed.

Then he got out again.

He had to go to
the bathroom.

SQUEAK!
went the
handle.

WHOOSH!
went the water.

BANG!
went the
door.

OOPS!

"Something went SQUEAK!"
said Dad.

"Something went **WHOOSH!**" said Mum.

"Something went **BANG!**" said Dad.

They jumped out of bed . . .

and tiptoed downstairs.

"Goodness, WHAT A MESS!"
said Mum and Dad together.

"Now I know who was going BUMP," said Mum.

"Someone who likes chocolate cake," said Dad.

They tiptoed upstairs

and looked
into Olly's room.

"OLLY!" said Mum and Dad.

But Olly was fast asleep . . .

. . . OOPS! not for long.